FROZEN

THE ICE GAMES

DISNEP PRESS

LOS ANGELES • NEW YORK

Written by Calliope Glass
Illustrated by the Disney Storybook Art Team
For information address Disney Press, 1101 Flower Street, Glendale, California 91201.
ISBN 978-1-4847-4772-8
F383-2370-2-15195
Printed in China
First Edition, September 2015
1 3 5 7 9 10 8 6 4 2
For more Disney Press fun, visit www.disneybooks.com

It was winter in Arendelle—the happiest winter in many years.

Princess Anna and Kristoff were inside, reading quietly in front of a roaring fire. Suddenly, the sound of children's laughter came through the open window. Anna put down her book and went to the window.

"Oh!" she said. "Come look, Kristoff. It's soooo cute!"

Kristoff joined Anna at the window. Three children were building a toboggan in the snowy courtyard below.

Kristoff smiled at the children, but Anna could see that he was thinking about something else.

"All right," Anna said. "Out with it. What's on your mind?"

"I'm just thinking about the Ice Games," Kristoff said. "I bet those kids are building that tobaggan for the big race. . . ."

"The Ice Games?" Anna asked. "What are those?"

"Every year on the winter solstice, ice harvesters and their families from all over the world gather on a glacier and hold the Ice Games," Kristoff explained. "It's supposed to be really fun."

Anna turned to Kristoff. "Supposed to be? Didn't you ever participate?"

Kristoff shook his head sadly. "I didn't have a lot of friends when I was a kid," he said. "I mean, I had Sven. And the trolls. But only humans are allowed to enter the Ice Games. And you have to have a team of three."

Later Anna told Elsa what Kristoff had said.

"You mean all these years Kristoff has wanted to go to the Ice Games and he hasn't been able to?" Elsa asked.

Anna nodded. "It was so sad to hear him talk about missing the games," she said. "So I was thinking—"

"That *we* should take Kristoff to the games this year!" Elsa finished for her, delighted. "The three of us can be a team!"

"Yes!" Anna said, hugging her sister. "I knew you'd get it!"

Anna and Elsa ran to tell Kristoff about their plan.
"You'd do that for me?" he asked, his face red.
"Of course!" Anna said cheerfully. "Every ice
harvester should get to go to the Ice Games!"

Anna and Elsa were gathering supplies for their trip when they ran into Olaf. "Hi, Anna! Hi, Elsa!" he said. "Where are you going?"

"We're taking Kristoff to the Ice Games," Anna explained.

"Oooh, can I come?" Olaf asked.

Elsa smiled. "Not this time, Olaf," she said. "We need you and Sven to stay here and take care of Arendelle."

With Arendelle in good hands, Anna, Elsa, and Kristoff set off for the Ice Games. When they arrived, Anna couldn't help staring at the group around her. She'd never seen so many ice harvesters in one place!

"Say," one of them said, pointing at Elsa, "isn't that the queen of Arendelle? I heard she has magic ice powers."

"No fair!" said another. "She'll use her powers to win the games!"

"I promise on my honor as queen that I will not use my powers in the games," Elsa said solemnly.

"Yeah, so back off," said a gruff voice. Anna turned to see a group of ice harvesters from Arendelle standing behind her. With them were the three children she had seen outside the palace window! Anna grinned. She loved that the people of Arendelle were so loyal to her sister.

ICE GA

"Our queen wouldn't cheat," the little girl from Arendelle said. "And she doesn't need to, anyhow."

It was true: Elsa didn't need to use her powers to win the first contest. She carved a gorgeous ice statue of the rock trolls using just a hammer and a chisel.

Next was Anna and Kristoff's event.

"I don't care what the event is. I know we're going to win!" Anna said.

"Couples ice-skating," the announcer boomed.

"Unless it's that . . ." Anna said, her heart sinking. She was a terrible ice-skater.

But Anna wasn't one to back down from
a challenge. She and Kristoff gave it their all,
swooping and speeding around the rink. Kristoff
managed a little jump, and Anna only fell down
nine times. They didn't win, but they had a lot
of fun trying . . . and they did manage to come in
third place.

That night Anna, Elsa, and Kristoff had dinner with the rest of the ice harvesters. As they ate, they discussed the Ice Games.

"With Elsa's first-place finish, and Kristoff and me coming in third in the ice-skating," Anna said, "we actually stand a chance of winning the Ice Games!"

"All we have to do is win the big toboggan race tomorrow," Kristoff added.

"Good luck!" Anna heard a small voice behind her say. She turned around to see the little girl from Arendelle.

"Thank you," Anna replied with a smile. "You made the ice sculpture of the palace today, right?"

The girl nodded, blushing furiously.

"It was beautiful," Elsa said. "And I know a little something about making ice palaces!"

Grinning from ear to ear, the little girl ran back to sit with her family.

"Good luck to you, too!" Anna called after her.

"What a sweet little girl," Elsa said. "She reminds me of someone else at her age."

"Me?" Anna asked hopefully.

"I said 'sweet,' Anna. Not 'annoying,'" Elsa replied with a wink.

Anna punched her sister playfully.

"Of course, I meant you, Anna," Elsa admitted.

"One more round of hot chocolate?" Kristoff suggested.

"Yes, please!" Anna and Elsa said together.

As the sun rose the next morning, Anna, Elsa, and Kristoff piled into their toboggan. It was time for the last event.

"Here we gooooooo!" Anna shrieked. The trio rocketed down the slope with the rest of the racers.

Anna squinted against the wind as their toboggan went faster and faster. Soon they had pulled ahead of the other racers. "We're winning!" she yelled.

Anna, Elsa, and Kristoff were almost to the finish line when another toboggan passed them. It was moving so fast they couldn't even see who was inside.

The toboggan streaked down the slope and across the finish line. It was the children from Arendelle!

"We won! We won!" the kids yelled, hugging each other and jumping up and down. Watching them celebrate, Anna couldn't bring herself to be disappointed that she, Kristoff, and Elsa hadn't won.

She just hoped Kristoff wasn't too upset.

"I'm sorry we didn't come in first, Kristoff," Elsa said later, as they took their place on the winners' podium.

Kristoff grinned. "Nah," he said. "Don't be. I finally got to compete in the Ice Games! And I think it's great that they won. Having friends you can count on is really important when you're a kid."

Anna hugged Kristoff. "Having friends you can count on is really important forever. And I have the best friends of all!"

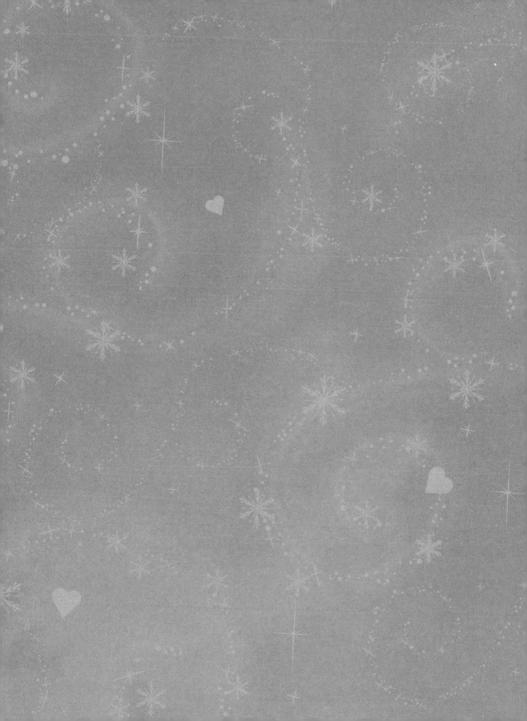